For Heather Prentice

Printed in Belgium

First U.S. Edition   1 2 3 4 5 6 7 8 9 10
Library of Congress Cataloging in Publication Data
Cooper, Helen (Helen F.)
The tale of bear / by Helen Cooper.
p.   cm. Summary: When he accidentally gets put in the washing machine,
Timothy's favorite old Bear is afraid that Timothy will not like him
because he looks different.
ISBN 0-688-13990-6 [1. Toys—Fiction. 2. Teddy bears—Fiction.
3. Stories in rhyme.] I. Title. PZ8.3.C785Tb 1995
[E]—dc20 94-21054 CIP AC

THE TALE OF
BEAR

HELEN COOPER

Lothrop, Lee & Shepard Books   New York

Whatever Timothy had to do,
Bear came too.
So wherever Bear was, there was Tim
next to him.

Bear began to feel quite scruffy.
His feet and fur were getting yucky.
Still, Timothy took him everywhere—
he didn't mind a dirty old Bear.

One morning Cat came in to play
and hid Tim's bear Bear on washing day!

Poor Bear got trapped in the washing machine,
sploshing around in the soap and steam.
"Won't someone help me!" shouted Bear,
but no one saw him tumbling there.

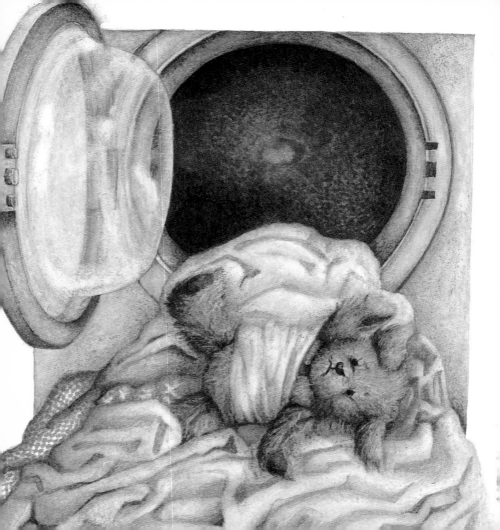

"Oh, no!" said Mom when she opened the door and Bear fell out on the kitchen floor.
He was soaked to his stuffing, and very scared that Tim wouldn't want a soggy old Bear.

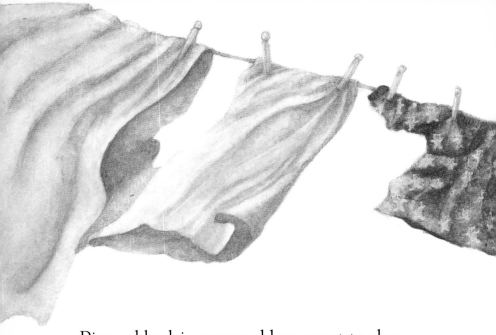

Pinned by his ears and hung out to dry,
wet and bedraggled, Bear wanted to cry.
He couldn't help worry, as he hung in the air,
that Tim wouldn't want a saggy old bear.

When he dried out and Mom brushed his hair,
he looked in the mirror—what a handsome bear!
Then he thought again and worried some more:
Would Tim like him better as he was before?

Tim was very surprised to find
his bear was clean, but he didn't mind.
Dirty paws or clean golden hair,
he loved his squashy old, saggy old Bear.